Illusions

or

Facts

A Collection of Spine-chilling Tales

By

Dr Shagun Thakur

& Dr Vikas Gurbani

Cover Design : Canva.com

First Edition : Aug 2022

Language : English (United States)

Ebook :

Kindle Direct Publishing (KDP) by Amazon

(World-wide publication)

Paperback :

1. KDP Amazon world-wide except India.
2. In India, Retail and Online Distribution through Pothi.com

About the Book

This book is a collection of eleven short stories from the Hills of Himachal Pradesh. The stories belong to various genres like Fiction/ Mystery/ Thriller/ Folklore/ Suspense/ Supernatural. The content ranges from the unnatural experiences of a person on a new job posting, to the story of a weeping mother who is allegedly back from the dead, for her child. It has various other stories of mysterious entities and phenomena.

About the Authors

Dr Shagun Thakur is working as a Faculty in a Medical College in Bhubaneswar. Born and brought up in the Kangra district of Himachal Pradesh, the concept and stories of this book are designed by her.

Dr Vikas Gurbani is working as a Faculty in a Medical College in Gujarat. He has contributed to this book by revising and editing the stories.

Dedicated To

The Almighty,

Ancestors and Elders,

Family,

And Friends

(Lord Balabhadra, Maa Subhadra, Lord Jagannath)

Painting by Dr Shagun Thakur

Preface

The stories in this book are about a girl child, Shakku, who is born and brought up in Himachal Pradesh. She lives with her mother, father and grandmother.

During her childhood she came across many stories narrated by her elders and also has certain unexplainable experiences of her own. The author/s have tried to present her experiences during various years of her childhood. The young girl is curious about the explanation of these incidents. The author/s have also tried to highlight how during her adulthood Shakku revisits those incidents and tries to see them from a different point of view. The stories are set in locations such as Shakku's home, neighboring farms, rivers and various other places in the land of Himachal.

Disclaimer

The book 'Illusions or Facts - A Collection of Spine-Chilling Tales' is a work of fiction. Names, characters, businesses, events and incidents are products of the author's imagination. Any resemblance to actual events or persons, living or dead, is entirely coincidental. The author/s do not intend to propagate any opinions or beliefs through the content of this book, neither do the authors support the same. The authors do not intend to hurt the sentiments of any religion or any faith.

Table of Contents

Story 1 - The Trickster (‘*Chaleda*’)

Shakku, a 14-year old girl residing in the hilly area of Kangra (Himachal Pradesh) was having her afternoon nap after a tiring morning at school. She had savored her favorite food items for lunch. Any paneer dish in food used to tempt her and she relished it whenever occasionally it was made at home. Home-made curd was her second favorite and a meal accompaniment on a daily basis. It used to infuriate her when she was not served curd during the night. "You will wake up sick in the morning," her mother used to tell her.

She cherished her walks - to and fro - from the school which she had to take in case she missed the school bus. The people in the hills are taught right from childhood how to carefully ascend and descend on the hills while walking. It was a good day for her as she had scored her best in the school examination. Her father had promised her that she would be rewarded with any of her wishes. In return, she took a promise from her father that he will give her company in playing video-games.

Being the lone child to her parents, Shakku always missed the company of a sibling at home. She lived with her mother (Sadho), father (Gilloo) and grandmother (Rani Devi). Her grandmother was fond of religious places and was on the tours most of the time, visiting places of interest. But Shakku enjoyed her time with her grandmother whenever she was home. Her "Amma" amazed her always with her fascinating stories. Her mother and father both were working in a Government School. Living in the lap of nature, she was fond of the birds-chirping, sounds made by various insects and the beautiful greenery in her surroundings.

She had a video-game of the 90s on which she enjoyed playing the "Tank" game but always felt it would have been better to play the game with a partner. Her father often promised her that he would give her company, but couldn't find time because of the various work commitments. It was her mother who gave her company most of the time. A growing child's mind is filled with curiosity and questions about everything, which in case of

Shakku, were addressed mostly by her mother and they had lots of conversations.

The clock hit 6 in the evening and Shakku's father had not returned from work. She was feeling depressed and angry at the same time and her anger was turning into a rage. She became furious and started shouting at her mother, "He always does this. One simple thing I asked and he didn't show up. Why does he even promise then?. Her mother tried to console her but was falling short of success.

Sadho (mother) came up with an idea and told Shakku, "Everytime when he returns, he finds us at home. But this time it will be different. Let him come and search for us and we will hide somewhere and be hard to reach. He will realize how angry we are with him on this one. I also have the same complaint from him. Why make a promise when you can't keep it." "Listen," she added "we both will leave the house and go far off so he can't find us. This will annoy him big time and we will have our revenge".

After hearing her mother, Shakku had a mischievous smile on her face. She loved this hide and seek game and as a kid liked her mother's idea. "Yes, let's do that," Shakku exclaimed. "It will take a long time for him to find us," Shakku thought in her mind. They didn't even tell Amma and left the home.

It was the month of September when the rains had just eased up but the chilling winter had not yet started. However, the weather was still pretty cold. Shakku was wearing her shawl over her t-shirt and pajamas. Sadho was wearing a full Punjabi suit which the ladies of Himachal usually wear consisting of a Kurta, Pajama and Dupatta; the dupatta draping her head.

All and all, it was a great time to enjoy the outdoors. Shakku and her mother went into the nearby wheat fields to hide from their father and walked across to the farthest field from the home. The large field of farming is chalked out into various squares for cultivation of crops. There are thin walk-ways between these squares which are not more than 2 ft wide. They were seated in those walk-ways such that only the top portion of their heads can be seen. The produce of this grain field had grown two to two and half feet in height and hence, it was difficult to spot someone who was seated in this field.

Both of them were seated in a place in a mischievous and playful mood waiting for Gilloo to come and search for them. They were talking about him raising various issues accusing him of not showing-up when needed. Sadho also narrated the times when even she had expectations from Gilloo but was left disappointed at the end. After venting out their anger for some time, both of them also realized how hard-working Gilloo is, and why due to the various activities that he has taken upon himself to keep the home running and fulfill everyone's wishes at home, he is unable to make it sometimes. The conversation shifted from criticism to praise.

The Sun was about to set. Sadho got a bit relaxed seeing her child calm down and enjoying their time together. It was then when Shakku noticed someone walking towards them from far away. From the silhouette she could make out that it was her father searching them and walking towards them. She pointed the same to her mother who was also happy to see that. Carrying on with their conversation about various things at home and school, Shakku, in a matter of few seconds, saw her grandmother and their dog walking towards them on the same path at quite a distance away. She and her mother thought that alright both Gilloo and Amma were searching for them and approaching them.

The mother and child duo got back to their conversation and after a few seconds, they saw a bull approaching towards them. After exchanging a few glances when they looked back again, an unknown person was walking towards them. This was now about 40-50 feet away. They shift their attention for a few seconds and now two strangers are approaching them. This was raising doubts in their mind. Another few seconds and they see three grown adult men sitting in the opposite field, smoking bidis (handmade tobacco cigarettes) and playing cards. All these switches or transformations were happening just when they were shifting their glance from site of occurence.

It was then when it hit Sadho's mind and she realized from her past knowledge and experiences what they were dealing with.

Without thinking much, Sadho kept both her hands on Shakku's shoulders and told her, "*Beta* (my child), stand up... Don't talk now and we will quietly walk home." Holding her calm, she continued, "If you hear your name in any voice don't look back and keep walking towards our home." Both of them headed towards their home at a pace. Sadho had told her child not to pay attention to any voices she hears and under no circumstances look back. Sadho was frightened but Shakku was confused as she could not make out the situation. But she followed her mother's heed and both of them were about to reach close to their home. On reaching home Gilloo was waiting eagerly for them.

Watching her wife and daughter covered in sweat and trying to catch a breath, he got more worried as to what had happened. Gilloo asks them in a startled voice, "What happened and where were you both". Gasping for breadth, Sadho vocalized, "*Chaleda... chaleda!*" (Trickster). "in the fields", she added. After heaving a sigh of relief, Sadho narrated the whole ordeal to Shakku's father. Gilloo understood and got hold of the situation. He went to the temple within the home premises and offered his prayings and was grateful to God that no untoward thing happened.

Among all these happenings, Shakku was left confused as to what just occurred and what is this 'Chaleda'. She asked her mother to tell her everything. Wondering how to explain the event to a child with an impressionable mind, she answered, "There are many stories about him and different people have different experiences and versions. This Chaleda entity is a *maayavi* (illusionist) which will appear in various disguises and show you different things from your mind. He can read your mind and will show you what he wants to show you. He will at first reveal himself in familiar appearances and then confuse you with things to trick your mind so that he can take you away with Him."

Intrigued by the story, Shakku asked, "Where is the world of Chaleda, where can he be found?". Sadho replied,"He cannot be found. He can only reveal himself to you if he wants to. He has many faces and also carries the souls of the people who have fallen to his deceptive charm."

Shakku was getting scared and she hurried to her grandmother's room slamming the door open. She told her grandmother what had conspired and asked her whether she knew anything about this entity. Rani Amma, seeing her child scared and fascinated at the same time, started narrating her own experience, "I was young and living in our residence whose renovation work had just started. I was sitting in my room on the first floor of the house, working on a house-hold chore, when a voice like that of my Aunt called my name. I ignored it at first and carried on with my chore but then I started hearing my name again and again, calling me outside. I started walking towards the voice in kind of an engrossed or hypnotized way when suddenly I fell from the first floor onto the ground floor. There was no boundary wall on the first floor as the construction was going on."

Shakku was stunned hearing her grandmother's narration and continued listening, "When I woke up, the people at home told me that my Aunt had not visited the house for many days. She lives in another village about 25 kms away from my home. My parents saw me lying on the ground and threw water on my face. After I came to my senses, I told my parents the whole ordeal."

Amma showed her scar on the forehead from the injury and Shakku was left speechless after hearing about the incident. Amma further conveyed to Shakku, "That's why, it is said that you should not pay attention to unfamiliar voices or foray into the unknown and uncharted territories."

Rani *Amma* continued, "Those who continue to look into his (*Chaleda's*) tricks get lost in his world and get hypnotized. They cannot be found and are reported missing. This is the chatter of the people in the village."

Shakku was a little confused now and was wondering if she is being told this so that she doesn't go out of home alone.

Shakku although never came across a similar experience in future but continues to live with the memories of it without any explanation of what had occurred. Shakku, in later years, thought her grandmother's story may be because of the head injury she suffered. The injury could have caused the confusional state leading her to believe that it was the trickster.But she could not comprehend what she had seen with her own eyes in the field. How come her mother and she herself had seen the same phenomenon in the field which could not be comprehended.

As an adult, Shakku came across mentions of entities like "Shape-shifter", "Drifter", allegedly reported in different works of fiction. She thought to herself whether this could be about the same entity which she had encountered as a child. Shakku had seen it with her own eyes and couldn't believe it was real. Can two people have the same illusion? If it was an illusion.

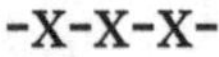

Story 2 - The New Posting

Shakku, in her 5th standard of school, was having a routine Saturday evening at home. Suddenly, her father entered the house with a bag of freshly chopped chicken. “What’s special tonight, Papa?” she merrily asked. “Your Dharmu Uncle is coming home, Beta (my child)” Gilloo replied. “He just got free from his new posting in Chamba District and is making a visit to our place,” he added.

Shakku was fond of her Dharmesh Uncle as he always had many joyful and laughter-filled stories to tell. During his visits, he often brought her favorite chocolate. Shakku had all the reasons to be excited with joy. Shakku’s father, Gilloo entered the kitchen to prepare the dinner.

Sadho, Shaku’s mother, wasn't used to assisting her husband on the non-vegetarian preparations. Sadho had taken up vegetarian food in her later years and hated the sight of meat. Gilloo had a good hand in the kitchen and used to prepare lip-smacking dishes when it came to cooking flesh.

Story 2 - The New Posting

Shakku, in her 5th standard of school, was having a routine Saturday evening at home. Suddenly, her father entered the house with a bag of freshly chopped chicken. "What's special tonight, Papa?" she merrily asked. "Your Dharmu Uncle is coming home, Beta (my child)" Gilloo replied. "He just got free from his new posting in Chamba District and is making a visit to our place," he added.

Shakku was fond of her Dharmesh Uncle as he always had many joyful and laughter-filled stories to tell. During his visits, he often brought her favorite chocolate. Shakku had all the reasons to be excited with joy. Shakku's father, Gilloo entered the kitchen to prepare the dinner.

Sadho, Shaku's mother, wasn't used to assisting her husband on the non-vegetarian preparations. Sadho had taken up vegetarian food in her later years and hated the sight of meat. Gilloo had a good hand in the kitchen and used to prepare lip-smacking dishes when it came to cooking flesh.

It was the rainy season and showers used to pour now and then. At 8.30 in the evening, Shakku heard the engine revving of the scooter and came to know that Dharmu uncle had arrived. Dharmu, a man in his 40s, wearing a gents kurta and pajama entered the home after removing his blue raincoat outside. Shakku greeted him with a traditional namaste and uttered, “Uncle, chocolate?”. Gilloo gave her daughter a disagreeable look and said her name in a way to manner her up. Dharmu smiled and took out a white milkybar chocolate, one of Shakku’s favorites, and gave it to her. “She’s a child, Gilloo ji, let her have it and enjoy her Uncle’s visit”, he told Shakku’s father.

Gilloo and Dharmu got seated on the sofa and started catching up on things. They were talking about the Dharmu’s new job posting in Chamba district which didn't interest Shakku much. She had found a half-burnt stick from the kitchen (wood used as cooking fuel) and was making drawings, with the burnt charcoal from one end of the stick, on the floor. After a few minutes, all of them sat for dinner and enjoyed the chicken made with home-made spices.

After dinner, as it was getting late, it was Shakku's time to go to bed. Sadho tried tucking her to bed but because of Dharmu's visit, she was in no mood to call off the day tonight. She started whining in response and uttered "I will sleep here itself on the sofa, on uncle's lap" and had her wish fulfilled. She closed her eyes and pretended to sleep so that no one will bother her again. But she had no idea what would follow.

Dharmu asked Gilloo about the things back at the hometown while he was away at his new job in Chamba. They were having their conversation and Gilloo noticed something and asked, "What are you thinking and hesitating to speak, Dharmu?". After a long pause, Dharmu replied, "Gilloo ji, I don't know how to share this one. I am very much shocked by an incident at the new quarters provided to me in Chamba. I am even frightened to go there again?" "What is it? Tell me" Gilloo asked again awaiting a reply. Shakku, lying there on the sofa with her eyes closed pretending she has fallen asleep, suddenly became attentive but didn't open her eyes. She had never heard her Uncle so tense for something. She had always known him as a jolly-good fellow.

Getting a hold of his thoughts, Dharmu said, "I am living in this society provided to me by my company. They have independent rooms for the staff to stay but the lavatories are shared and few in number." "Hmmm" Gilloo nodded. Dharmu continued, "In the morning hours particularly at 5 am, there's a rush of residents to use the washrooms. He also had the routine of getting up at the same time and answering nature's call. It was a similar routine every morning and he was getting used to the new place. During his visits, he used to notice a lady using the lavatory at the same time, 5 AM. She used to wear a saree with a '*Ghoongat*' (part of saree) covering her head, so I never got a chance to see her face."

Gilloo was paying attention and listening to Dharmu's narration and even Shakku was a silent audience of the event. Dharmu continued, "On one insignificant morning, I saw the same lady entering the lavatory but didn't see her coming out. Half an hour had passed and I got worried as to whether she is okay or needs any help. So, I knocked at the door but nobody answered and after a few moments I found that the door was not locked from inside and I pushed it gently. To my surprise, there was no one inside."

"I was amazed and I asked the peon, Ramu, an elderly man, on the society premises and told him about the incident. Do you know what I found out?" Dharmu said. "What?" Gilloo asked curiously to know where this is all going. Dharmu answered, "The peon told me that as per my description there was a widow who used to stay there and used the washroom at that time in the morning. She had gone missing for a week and nobody noticed. After a week, her decomposed dead body laid with maggots was found in her room. The Police investigation couldn't uncover what had happened."

Gilloo was stunned to hear how the story had been uncovered. Shakku, who was hiding behind her sleep, was also shocked to hear about the incident. It was too much for a child to be exposed to such an incident. She had never seen Dharmu uncle in such a state of mind before. Resisting any response, she continued her pretension of sleeping. Dharmu continued with his narration, "Ramu further told me that some other residents of the society have also had similar experiences. Many still see her following a daily routine. But she hasn't harmed anyone till date."

Taking a breath, Dharmu added,"But what shook me to core was that the next day Ramu was found dead inside the same bathroom, reported to be dying of a heart attack." Shakku started sobbing now and that's when the men realized she had overheard the whole ordeal. Dharmu gave a gentle smile and told Shakku, "See, this is your punishment. That's why I told you this frightening story so that you don't stay awake late hours. Now, go to your room and sleep on your bed". Sadho who was also a witness to all the happenings now took Shakku to her room to sleep.

Shakku held on to that story for many years. During her college days, she asked her father again about the story- as to what had actually occurred -was it true or just a piece of fiction. Her father told her that the incident had actually happened and Dharmu uncle was not lying. The death of the peon due to the heart attack and the existence of the widow earlier were all true. She pondered hard whether the death of the peon was a coincidence? Was the lady just a creation of Dharmu's mind?

Story 3 - Suffering Dairy Farmer

Chir pine or Longleaf Indian pine, is a species of trees which is native to the Himalayas. These Blue Pine trees are found in the districts of Kangra and Una in Himachal Pradesh. The younger pine trees are usually conical, with whorls of horizontal branches whereas their older counterparts may have round, flat, or spreading crowns.

Shakku was raised in a village surrounded by hills covered by these beautiful pine trees. The homes in her village were sparsely spaced with a lot of open areas. Many homes had their own farm fields attached with the house.

Having warm milk in the cold winters was something Shakku enjoyed right since her childhood. She savored the various products made from milk like curd, paneer, ghee and buttermilk. Her grandmother was a believer of 'black magic' (occult sciences) and never sourced milk from outside, particularly the local milkman, Gogi.

She tried as much as possible to see that the goods consumed in the house are sourced from their own fields and the farm animals. She even bought a cow so that they don't have to buy milk from the local dairy farmer.

Shakku enjoyed the company of this new family member named 'Gaura' in her courtyard. It was a brown color cow, with a distinct white patch on its left horn. The young girl had found a much needed company but her mother, Sadho, got into trouble taking care of this messy member of the house. Sadho also had a day job working as a School Teacher in a School. When Gaura started giving milk, it fulfilled all the dairy needs of the family and more was left to distribute among the relatives, the close neighborhood and even Sadho's work colleagues.

One day *Amma* (Rani Devi), seated in her bed, called Sadho. Shakku also went along to see what was the matter. Shakku's grandmother started boasting about her decision of buying a cow and how fruitful it has proved. She told Sadho, "Do you know why I brought Gaura home?" "No," Sadho replied, "why?" *Amma* told her, "The dairy farmer from whom you buy milk has a certain knowledge of occult sciences. He has been suffering for a long time and there have been a lot of complaints regarding him." "What do you mean, kindly tell me?" Sadho asked inquisitively.

Amma then narrates the following chain of events.

The villagers have been complaining regarding the milk supplied by the dairy farmer to them. There were instances where the people after consuming the milk turned ill. The villagers first thought the milk could have been infected and hence the resulting illness. But one person after drinking the milk went into seizures. On regaining consciousness, he reported that he saw some man choking him and saying, "How dare you have the milk which is on my property?" A similar incident later happened with a lady residing in the village. She said that man told him, "I will not only destroy you but will also kill Gogi (the local dairy farmer)". Slowly all these stories fell on the ears of Gogi whose business was suffering because of such incidents and getting worse day by day.

The people started flocking Gogi's house to get answers. They questioned him whether he had harmed anyone or was involved in any wrongdoing. Gogi in his teary eyes sitting on the ground tells them disheartenedly, "In the past eight months I have lost six buffaloes to death and four others are presently ill. I even consulted a veterinary surgeon for the same and is following whatever he has suggested but things are not getting better."

One of the villagers, looking at the plight of the milkman, thought that there could be more to the story than what meets the eyes. He suggested the milkman consult a *Yogi* (spiritual healer). A Yogi living in a distant village was now approached by the suffering dairy farmer.

The Yogi heard the farmer's ordeal and seeing the condition of the farmer, understood how it was difficult for Gogi to make ends meet in these troubled times. He realized that if the farmer loses the four remaining animals also, then there will be no end to his suffering. He agreed to help in the matter and asked Gogi to bring a handful of soil from his farm where the animals are kept. Gogi obeyed the advice and returned to the Yogi with the soil taken from the place where his farm animals used to stay.

The Yogi took the soil in his palm and clenched it. He then closed his eyes and went into a ruminative state. After pondering on it for twenty odd minutes, he opened his eyes with an enlightened smile. He asked Gogi, "Do you have an old big Peepal (Sacred Fig) tree near your house?" Gogi was surprised to hear that and answered positively. Gogi added, "It lies in front of my courtyard where I tie my buffaloes" The Yogi further enquired, "Does the tree have a branch extending towards your house?" Gogi said, "Yes, from the past few months, there is an outbranching in the direction of the courtyard".

The Yogi continued, "Now listen to me very carefully. The shadow of that branch of the tree is falling on the place where the buffaloes are kept. In that tree resides a *Jin* (Jeanie) and feels the Tree is his home. He is also of the belief that wherever the shadow of the tree falls, it's his place. If you cut the tree, he will definitely destroy your house too. So you can't cut the tree but you can cut the branch which is extending into the courtyard which he can't claim or harm you. The *Jins* pray at 4.00 am in the morning. This is the time when you will have to do the act. The Jin will be deeply engrossed in his prayers and won't notice the act."

Hearing a solution to his problems, a new rush of life entered Gogi's exhausted body. He registered everything the Yogi said in his mind and returned home with the decision to do the act the very next day. At sharp 4 A.M. in the morning, he severed the branch of the Peepal tree outgrowing his courtyard."

Shakku's grandmother concluded the story by saying, "His farm animals started getting healthy after doing the remedy suggested by the Yogi."

A few moments later, Amma made a frightened and somewhat sad face and said, "When I came into this home after my marriage, my mother-in-law had told me about this tree. She said that in this particular Peepal tree earlier, the villagers had nailed a jin who was harming the residents of the village. So, never cross its shadow as it can reign you and harm you."

Later, to Shakku's surprise, she found that even her father had heard all these stories about the *Peepal* tree and the *Jin*. She thought it to be natural as her grandmother has raised his father so he must be hearing these tales right from childhood. His father told him that while playing near the Tree during childhood, his friends felt someone was calling them by name. Whey they would gaze from where the sound came or ask others, nobody used to own it up.

Rani Devi (Amma) was feeling fortunate that she never happened to be any part of the incidents related to the Tree. Shakku continued to wonder, whether these stories were a piece of fiction or were they facts?

Story 4 - The Bird-chirp

Himachalis (People of Himachal Pradesh) live in the lap of nature surrounded by lush-greenery, various biological species including birds, insects, animals and a lot of biodiversity.

In Himachal Pradesh, the *'Sair'* festival is celebrated in the month of September. It is known as the *"Bada-din"* (Big day) of the hillmen. It falls just before the start of the cold winter. *'Sair'* is actually the name of a local insect which, when seen around, marks the beginning of this festival. On this day, the people worship their local deity for a prosperous future and delicious food is prepared at home.

The state bird of Himachal Pradesh is Jujurana or Western tragopan, which is a brightly plumed bird endemic to the northwest Himalayan region. It belongs to the family of pheasants.

Shakku was fascinated by the various species of birds spotted in her neighborhood, as she was growing up. She was in her 3rd standard at school when the following occurred. One afternoon, she was seated in the courtyard of her home with her grandmother, Rani Devi. Her *Amma* (grandmother) was cooking the lunch on the traditional stonemade stove (with wood as fuel) and she was enjoying a serving of homemade aam-papad (sweet mango pickle). Rani *Amma's* pickles were very famous among her relatives and also people close to the family. She made a variety of pickles all year around and stored them in glass jars. Everyone wanted to get their hands on any one or more of these jars.

While Shakku was enjoying her favorite delicacy, she heard the chirp of a bird which sounded like *"jaunsaurya.."* Curious as to the type of sound produced, she asked her grandmother, "What is that sound? What is the bird saying, Amma?" Keeping her cooking scoop down on the vessel lid, her grandmother answered, "*Beta* (child), she is uttering *jaun saurya, i.e., ghar jaun kya saurya* (Can i go home, father-in-law)." She continued, "This bird is actually the reincarnation of the newly-wedded bride". "What newly-wedded bride, *Amma*?" Shakku asked curiously. Then her *Amma* told her the following story.

The tale is of a lady who had just arrived at her in-laws house. It had been a few months after her wedding and she was missing her parental home. She missed her father and was remembering how he always fulfilled all her wishes at half-said words. The memories of her mother brought tears to her eyes when she remembered how she used to make her a sweater every winter season and the way she praised her at every achievement she made. This made her homesick and she eagerly wanted to visit her parent's home.

After marriage, she got so occupied in taking care of her husband and in-laws that she never got time to think about all this. Adjusting to the new place and new people is difficult for every bride. After a few months in the new house and adapting to the new measures, she got time to ponder on her old home. This was making her feel low.

One day, she made up her mind to ask permission from her father-in-law (saurya, sasurji) for the visit. Dressed in a traditional suit and covering her head with a *palloo* (portion of dupatta), she approached her father-in-law and requested, "*Ghar jaun saurya* (Can i go home father-in-law). It's been many months since i have been to my native place. Can I make a visit with your permission?"

The father-in-law thought to himself, "She has been taking care of us and managing everything in the household. How will things run in the house without her? I can't even deny her as this is the first wish she has made in the past months post her marriage." Thinking long and hard, he replied, "Sure dear, just take care of one more chore before you leave for your home. Kindly fill the water-storage container of the house so that it will be convenient for us when you are not here. Then you can make preparations for your home-visit."

Hearing the reply, the bride was pleased and there was no end to her joy. She nodded in reply and before doing the last chore which was asked by her father-in-law, she went to her room. It took her a while to really believe the news and make up her mind regarding the things she will pack to take with her.

Little did she know that there was something else brewing in her father-in-law's mind. Her father-in-law was not in favor of the newly wed leaving home. He and others in the home were too dependent on her to let her go even for a few days. He made a pin-head sized hole in the clay pots which she was going to use to carry the water back home. There were no pipelines for water that time and no nearby wells also. The water had to be sourced from the nearby river.

Getting back to her senses after the happy news, she decided to finish the chore and start packing for the trip. She took the array of pots and went to fill them from the nearby water source.

It was afternoon and everyone home had just finished their lunch half an hour back. After filling her pots, when she returned home, her father-in-law told her, "Good, you got us water. Let's see how much you have got. Will it suffice." When the lady unloaded the pots, to her surprise, they were almost empty with no water in them. She couldn't believe her eyes. "How will we manage with this dear? I just asked you one thing. Go back and get them filled".

When she returned after filling them, the same thing occurred again and she couldn't make out what was happening. Why are the filled pots turning empty on returning home. It was getting late in the evening and she also had to make the necessary arrangements for the trip back home. But the cruel father-in-law did not budge from his decision and asked her to get the pots filled again.

She kept doing it without knowing about the leak in the pots. She was desperate to go home at the same time. The sun was setting and she made increasing efforts to finish the task in the desire of visiting her home. Every time she came back, she asked her father-in-law the same question and he replied with the same condition.

The ordeal continued till finally the bride was completely exhausted and gave up her last breath in the courtyard trying hard to complete this physically daunting task. Her last words were the same,

"Saurya gharyo jaun" (Can i go home, father-in-law).

The bird chirping *"jaunsaurya.."* is the reincarnation of this bride who lost her life in a want of visiting home.

Shakku was amazed to hear her grandmother's narration of the story. She wondered whether this story of reincarnation is true or is it just made up to tell the ordeal of every newly-wedded bride who longs to visit her home. She thought it could be a folklore which the elderly ladies in the family narrated to their daughters and granddaughters. The story stayed with her into her adult years and with the question that, was it really a fact?

–x–x–x–

Story 5 - Pahadiya

Growing up in the hilly areas of Himachal Pradesh, Shakku was fascinated by the tales which she used to hear from her grandmother, mother and other close relatives. Being a child with a curious mind, these stories made her question reality. She used to find it difficult connecting the dots sometimes.

One more such incident stayed in her mind for years after hitting adulthood also. This was about an entity, well-known locally as 'Pahadiya' (A Mysterious God) whom many used to follow and many used to fear.

In her childhood, she asked her grandmother,"Amma, what is this Pahadiya everyone talks about?" Rani Devi explained to her, "It is an entity which resides in the Peepal (Sacred Fig) tree. It is a tall being and always wears white clothes as he loves the color white. Therefore, the people who worship this local deity, make their offerings in white, like white flowers, white flags and white khichdi (a semi-liquid preparation of rice) or anything which is white in color. At night, no one should go close to the tree as it makes him angry even at the slightest provocation."

Shakku became intrigued with this entity. She had heard of it from many sources - some shared their own experiences and others had tales to tell which they themselves overheard from somewhere. A few months later, one incident happened which involved the Pahadiya and Shakku was also part of the story.

It was the month of January and the whole State was in the celebration of the festival of *Lohri*. *Lohri* is a popular winter folk festival or the harvest festival of farmers celebrated in Northern India. It commemorates the passing of the Winter Solstice and looks forward to longer days as the sun journeys towards the northern hemisphere. The festival is celebrated by singing local rhymes gathered around bonfires. The people, particularly kids, visited other homes collecting sweets and produce of the farm, singing local folk songs and even performing traditional dance moves. The festivities continue late into the night.

On this day, at least one member of the family is seated at the entrance of the house with the sweets and farm produce (grains) to be distributed to whoever visits the home. On one such festival night, Shakku's parents had gone to sleep and she was given the charge of distributing the sweets and grains. Shakku sat in the courtyard wearing a Pattu (hand-made shawl) over her Indian suit and with the home-made sweets by her side in a container. She had her book with her to read and prepare for the upcoming exams. She was seated close to the *chulhah* (stone-made stove with wood as fuel) which was providing the warmth on this chilly winter night.

Many kids from the village visited her home. They greeted her, sang local hymns, exchanged conversations, collected the delicious sweets and some grains too. A small change of money is also given to the kids along with the consumables. One kid from the neighborhood was so happy to receive a nice sum of money that he made a repeat visit that night. But during his second visit Shakku just gave her some sweets and grains. She politely refused to give him cash again.

There was a *Peepal* (Sacred Fig) tree close to her house which was clearly visible from the area where she was seated. The rustling-swishing sound of the leaves was clearly audible in the silent hilly areas near Shakku's home. There was a sudden gush of winds and the rustling sound of leaves became louder. This was followed by all the birds which were resting on the nearby trees, flying away. She felt a chill in the spine and tried hard to ignore what she just saw. She was munching on a serving of peanuts and continued to do the same thinking this was just a normal thing to happen. Just when she tried continuing to be at peace, she noticed a group of kids coming towards her home.

There was a beautiful girl, 16-18 yrs of age, with her two younger brothers. One of them was roughly 12 year old and the other around 9 years old. All of them sat in Shakku's courtyard with her. They were there for quite some time and were getting to know each other. There was an exchange of conversations and sweets. All this was happening in the ongoing festive mood. After a few minutes, they left to visit another home and carry on with the festivities.

While they were crossing the Peepal Tree, Shakku saw something and could not believe her eyes. She couldn't figure out if it was an illusion or a reality. She saw a white silhouette near the Peepal Tree and the girl fainted. Her brothers started shouting for help. As there were not many homes nearby, Shakku woke up her father Gillooo from sleep. It was 3 am in the night. Both of them rushed to the place of incidence. The girl was lying in a pale condition and her younger brothers were worried about her and felt helpless. Shakku's father accompanied the trio to the nearby doctor's house.

Shagun returned to her home and went to sleep with her mother. She had no explanation for what she had seen with her own eyes and started to think whether the *'Pahadiya'* entity could be behind all this. The next few days were hard for her and she was not getting any updates on the condition of the girl.

Few days later, one of her friends told her, "The 16-year old girl is being treated in a mental hospital. After that night, the poor victim started complaining of a man dressed in white, not leaving her alone. He is saying that he will take her with him to the tree as he was mesmerized by her beauty."

At this juncture, Shakku got confused and afraid as to whether the thing she had seen that night had really occurred. She needed answers. She asked her father stubbornly to throw more light on the incident. The thought about where the girl is and what has happened to her didn't let her rest. She wanted to see the girl and asked her father to take her to the girl's place. Shakku's father agreed to her daughter's request as a father would not like to see his child in a disturbed condition.

He accompanied Shakku to the girl's house and requested her parents to allow his daughter to meet the girl. The girl's parents obliged and Shakku was taken to her room. Shakku found the girl in a very ill-looking condition. She had grown very weak. She mustered the courage to ask the girl about the incident and directly came to the point without much fuss. The girl replied, " Yes, I saw the *Pahadiya* that night and continue to see it till date. Our Baba (mystic healer) has assured me that he will make him go away."

Not just that. A few moments later, the girl uncovered her abdomen and showed Shakku, "See, it has even got me pregnant. See my tummy". Shakku being a child also could make out that the girl's abdomen was too distended for a 16-year old and that too with the rest of body being very thin.

Suddenly, the room's door opened and the girl's younger brother, a 9 year old, entered. "Give me a chocolate", he asked her sister. "Go away and don't bother me. If you come back again, I will tell the *Pahadiya* to teach you a lesson" she replied in an angry voice. The younger brother smiled cunningly and said, "I know Gautam *bhaiya*(brother) is your *Pahadiya* and because of him your abdomen has turned like this". He rushed outside after saying this and the girl tried to chase him. But seeing Shakku's father outside in the living room, she returned to her bed and sat with Shakku.

A few months later, the young pregnant girl gave birth to a child. Things started to become clear. Shakku came to know that Gautam was indeed the father of the child and the child was completely human to her relief. She fainted that night because of the pregnancy.

But Shakku couldn't explain the white silhouette she herself had seen that night. Was it an illusion or a fact?

Story - 6 Fires of The Angry Soul

Shakku's maternal aunt resided in the town of Baijnath in the Kangra district of Himachal Pradesh. The town is famous for an ancient temple of Lord Shiva. It is in this place where Ravana worshiped Lord Shiva and offered his ten heads in the havan kund (yagna).

Pleased by his worship Lord Shiva offered him the powers of immortality. During the Dussehra Festival in which an effigy of Ravana is traditionally burnt to celebrate the victory of Lord Rama over Ravana, symbolizes the victory of Good over Evil. But this ritual is not followed in the town of Baijnath because Raavana had worshiped Lord Shiva at this place and the Lord was pleased by his acts.

Shakku, currently 10 years old, came to know from her maternal aunt that the town is in news for a particular incident in a house and in its nearby areas, apparently where the things are catching fire without any source of ignition. The incident was in the local newspapers and the Police personnel were investigating the case. But in their investigation, the

Police also could not find how these flames were igniting.

These fire outbreaks were responsible for damaging the owner's property and causing menace in the area. The repeated incidents became the talk of the whole town and everyone wanted to know the mystery behind it. One house was particularly found to be at the center of all this matter.

This house was close to Shakku's maternal aunts' place. In this house resided an elder married brother and her young beautiful sister who was in her early 20s. The married brother had a wife and two children making it a family of five. The younger sister was having a charming appearance. She even had a characteristic small mole over her lip which seemed as if someone had made a dot with black pen and she was the one who had this a story explaining the events in her house.

On questioning by a neighbor she told him, "Few days back before any of this fire incident occurred, I was returning back to my house. As you know, to reach my house I have to take the path of railway tracks, where that night some young guys, around three in number, with an average build, asked me the route to Kheer Ganga which was nearby."

[Kheer Ganga is a river which flows through this area and is of religious importance. After carrying out the final rites of a person as per the Hindu tradition, the ashes are immersed in it to attain salvation, as taught by the ancestors of this place. The people who can't visit Haridwar for Asthi Visarjan (immersion of funeral pyre remains in holy rivers), they do it in Kheer Ganga of Baijnath.]

"So there are these three guys, in their mid-twenties asking for the route to it. I behaved like any good native would, and told them about the route to Kheer Ganga. Just when I was finished explaining, suddenly I saw some young white girl figurine floating towards me and I lost my consciousness. When I woke up, I noticed an hour had passed. There was no sign of those three guys but their bag was left there."

She continued, “In a confused state after regaining my consciousness, I saw this woman figure standing in front of the bag saying, "How dare you give them information about the route. These are my mortal remains (in the bag) and those three murdered me brutally. You are participating in their felony by letting me go without punishing them.” “Shocked by the sudden turn of events, I ran home and informed my brother who asked me to forget about the incident, suggesting that I must have seen all this in my dream. But then everyday this angry soul visited her by igniting fire and destroying property.”

The family did not want to be the laughing stock by telling this story to the investigating authorities. However, after seeing the mysterious fires in the house, they had to do something or approach someone who could help them. Hence, they approached a Sadhu Baba (Spiritual Healer) who lived in a far away forest area and many talked about his knowledge of the beyond.

When they narrated the whole thing to him, he called the angry soul to everyone's surprise. Fire ignited in a tree in front of him and the sister started making sounds which were supernatural.

Now the Sadhu Baba asked, " Who are you? Why are you causing this destruction and troubling innocent people". A woman's voice answered in a harsh sound, "She helped them! She helped the men who tortured me and wanted to get rid of me by immersing my remains in Kheer Ganga and thus, giving me salvation .

I am not ready for salvation!

I want revenge!"

The Sadhu asked the voice, "What revenge? What happened to you?"

She started crying and described the horrors she faced just before her death.

The angry soul in the unmarried sister's body now narrated her painful and sad story, "I was a young girl pursuing my college degree. I was on my way to buy a new suit in Baijnath market for the annual college freshers' party. I lived in a nearby village 20 km from the market so as I was walking on the road these three guys riding on the motorcycle approached me. They started eve-teasing and I asked them to leave me alone. The road was deserted with no help around and there was a dense forest on both the sides.

They parked their bike and dragged me deep in the woods and first threatened to kill me if I did not follow their instructions. They kept me there for 5 days, one of them will go home and two stayed with me taking turns. During this period, they did many cruel and monstrous acts on me. On my last night, one of them after drinking, broke the alcohol bottle and then stabbed me and kept on mutilating my body while I was alive. I could not take the pain and died crawling on the muddy floor. Then they burned me and left.

But I didn't leave them and my soul haunted them. When they realized that I was present after my death also, they decided to immerse my remains to get rid of me and this foolish girl was helping them. So, I took possession of her body and they ran fearing me leaving my remains which no one will find until you help me reach my oppressors and punish them."

The Sadhu after hearing this told her, "No, It's God's duty to punish, not yours!" and asked the family to find the remains and immerse them in Ganga. The figurine roused high in anger and as if it walked inside the Sadhu. As this occured, the Sadhu fainted and the family ran from there and went home. After that day, no fire ignited any more in the house or nearby areas. It seemed the angry soul had now trapped the Sadhu or maybe the Sadhu dealt with it - Who knows. Truly speaking, no one had the guts to solve the mystery further or attract the soul towards them by any means, since everyone in town had seen its wrath.

So in conclusion, no one knows whether the soul got what it wanted or it still lurks somewhere or it attained salvation.

In her adult years, when Shakku looked back on this story, she thought it can be a fictional story created to mask some one's medical condition in family that was Pyromania (irresistible desire to put things on fire) but how can I explain when so many people saw the ignition without any source of its own.

Mysterious Fire! - Illusion or Fact.

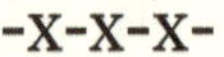

Story 7 - Bataali in the Kund

There are many natural water harvesting *kunds* (water caves) in the Himalayas. Sometimes they are underground and sometimes partly on the surface and the water drips into the water body. It has an opening through which water flows through the hill in winter and in summer it dries out to its bottom.

[A water cave is formed between the layers of the rock. The current of the river dissolves the joints, cutting it down and making its way through the rock layers. It ultimately opens in a cave which is partly air-filled.]

People enjoy swimming inside them as they are fascinated by these water caves under a rock which gives one shade. There is usually a small congested cave which is connected to these water caves. These congested caves no one dares to explore - their origins or what resides inside them. So it's a mystery how the water is brought into the water caves. One can hear the water dripping from rock from upward and water streaming from the cave making a distinctive sound.

During the rainy season, the sound of water dribbling by the rock is mesmerizing to hear. It was one of Shakku's happy places to visit. Shakku had heard that in these places lurks a supernatural creature which the *Pahadi* (hilly) people call *Bataali*. It resides in *kunds* (water caves) and travels along these congested caves.

First Shakku used to think it is just some reptile or any animal which somehow they describe, who takes away anyone going deep in the water-caves. But then something happened which changed her outlook towards any waterbody around.

Shakku was visiting her maternal grandparents' house at Sansai in Kangra district of Himachal Pradesh. At their place, these types of waterbodies are plenty in number. One of them is very large and is near to the place where all farm animals of her maternal grandparents are kept. Her grandmother had advised her to visit these places under the supervision of elders only. So, whenever she wanted to play in the kund, putting her feet inside water and enjoying it, her maternal grandmother warned her of an entity which would take her underwater.

At that time Shakku was an adolescent in her 8th class of school and felt her grandmother is just making up a story to prevent her from drowning and there is no entity called *Bataali.* So she ignored her advice and kept on playing. Enjoying her time in nature's lap, suddenly Shakku felt something touching her feet. She got scared and immediately pulled out her feet. She thought maybe *Nani's* (maternal grandmother) narration of the mystical creature took a toll on her mind and the incident could be having a simple explanation like the touching of the feet to fish swimming in water or any aquatic plant or weed.

The young curious child went to her great grandmother and asked her what was this *Bataali.* Her grandmothers' narration left her fearful because of which she could not enjoy any water-cave later in her life.

She narrated that this entity can't have off-springs on its own. So it takes a human as a breeding host, preferably girls. It lays eggs inside her, as the young girls have hormones which help its eggs to survive and mature. When the eggs grow and hatch, the host usually loses its life in the process and is used as a feed. However, if the host (victim) survives the horror, then *Bataali* can leave the victim back at the place from where he had brought her. The host (victim) does not have an entire recollection of events in her memory but only flashes of it. Inside the water where the breeding is taking place, the host's body is submerged in water with only the head above the water surface so she can breathe. The place is also pitch-dark as there is no source of light inside the cave.

On hearing this, Shakku's next question was about its appearance. To which her grandmother replied that it appears as human but instead of human skin, *Bataali* has crocodile-like skin or scales over its body.

Shakku's queries grew further and she asked whether this *Bataali* is a male or a female. Her grandmother answered that it is mostly female but males also exist. She further added that the male is rarely spotted but whoever has seen one says that a male *Bataali* can grant them a wish. Whatever the person who saw him asks, the *Bataali* grants them. The male *Bataali* grants wishes as they feel guilty for the actions of their female counterparts.

At this point of the story Shakku starts wondering about what wish she should ask if she is lucky enough to witness a male *Bataali*. Her grandmother further told her, "Sometimes he takes beautiful girls along with him to make his partner and he is actually loving and caring." Hearing this Shakku stopped pondering on what wish to ask for. She started regretting her previous wish. Her grandmother continued, "So don't go near these *kunds* as they are dangerous and never visit them alone.

Shakku, known for her notorious nature, went again near the large water cave all alone. It was raining that day and with all the new information with which she was enlightened, sat with her feet immersed in the water. She was a bit fearful thinking that if the story of this entity is true then what? As she was pondering on her thought, she saw some hairy structure coming out from a small end of the congested cave, from where the water was flowing. The entrance of the cave was right in front of her. She screamed in surprise and ran to her grandmothers' house, leaving her slippers behind and didn't dare to look back.

After reaching home and catching her breath, she thought to herself maybe it was just her imagination which made her see her fears. She had friends of her age in the neighborhood and felt like asking them about this *Bataali* being. A boy of her age told her that whatever she has heard is real.

He further narrated, 'My aunt was taken by a *Bataali* and returned after a year. When she came back, she was weak and mentally unwell. She repeatedly used to say that she has two children and she wants them. After a year when she came back to her senses, she said that she was taken into a cave by a female *Bataali.* There she was well-fed with fresh-water fishes and certain water weeds which were sweet and full of nutrition. *Bataali* had placed eggs inside her but when they were placed, she had no memory of it."

Shakku couldn't believe her ears and questioned him, "Did you believe all this what your aunt was saying?". He answered, "Not at first. But then I saw my aunt going to the kund every alternate day and bringing stones which were unusual to find in any pond. She kept them safe in the jewelry box."

He continued, "Not only this. After 4 months, she gave birth to a baby which died immediately but the scary thing was that the baby was not exactly human. It had scales all over its body. My aunt gave the explanation that three eggs were placed inside her. Two of them matured in time and hatched out to be normal. She gave a promise to *Bataali* to visit it from time to time and give her the children she was carrying. Keeping her promise. She gave two healthy male *Bataali* born to her on a previous occasion which she concealed and gave birth in water. Hence, she visited the *kund* for so many times. She had given birth in each month and the precious stones were the gift by *Bataali* to the lady for helping it have the desired offspring. But one which was weak, took time and again could not survive and died. This was seen by village people because it was born suddenly. Before this incident, many people in the neighborhood thought that the *Bataali* thing was just a hoax, but seeing all this they started believing that this entity might actually be in existence."

In her later years, Shakku thought that all this could just be a story to hide the phenomenon of loss of pregnancy or conceal the birth of a child born with congenital anomalies. The woman under consideration had become pregnant for the sixth time. All the fetuses were dead-born. She was being labeled as a bad omen or unfortunate being by her family. After her third dead-born child, she went and people started saying that *Bataali* took her.

Shakku found the explanation later that she tried getting pregnant again and delivering a child in a different place/village and lost two more children there. It was disheartening for her husband and the lady went into postpartum psychosis. Her husband brought her back home telling everyone this story. He wanted to distract the people and buy time for his wife to overcome the grief of her six lost pregnancies. The truth was very painful for the lady and her husband wanted that the story would give her certain calmness and peace in believing that she had given birth to two children who survived but were taken away by *Bataali* and are with him.

Sometimes we need illusions to survive the facts (reality).

Shakku also found out in her later years that there is a rare medical condition known as Harlequin Ichthyosis in which the whole body of the newborn is covered in fish-like scales. It is a genetic disorder. The child born with congenital anomaly could be having this condition.

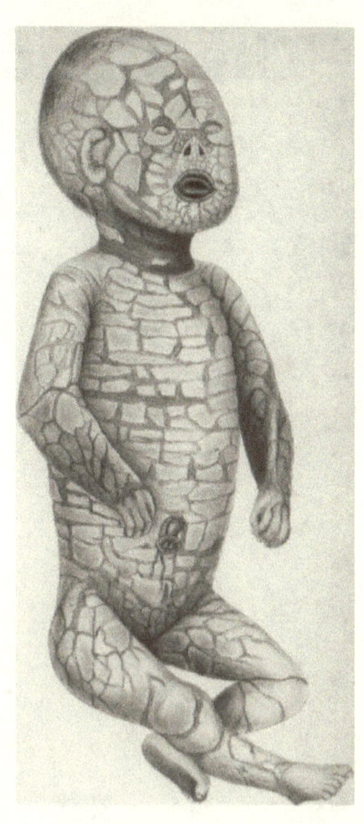

Infant with Harlequin-type Ichthyosis.

(Pic Source : Wikipedia)

Story 8 - The Mandh River

Shakku was brought up in a place filled with various forms of life - the plantations, the animals, and various species of birds close to the river source. Nature was closely perceived in every sense and it felt like one is living right in the lap of nature. Watching different types of insects crawl, a caterpillar hatching from its cocoon, a trail of ants moving and other wonders of nature mesmerized one with the creativity of God. At night the sounds of the various nocturnal wildlife kept Shakku company who didn't feel alone hearing these peaceful echoes.

The famous Beas river originates in the central regions of Himachal Pradesh and flows for around 470 kilometers to the Sutlej river in the Indian state of Punjab. It rises above sea-level at the Rohtang pass in Kullu. It traverses the Mandi district and then enters the Kangra District. The bed of this river is made up of unique white to grayish white stones of various shapes and sizes. Because of the continuous flow of water, these stones don't have sharp edges. They are even used for decoration in homes and because of trade they also make their way out of Himachal Pradesh and are seen in various homes across India and abroad.

The river crosses near Shakku's village and it is known as Mandh River in her area. Shakku enjoyed her evenings, walking on the banks of this river and collecting small white pebbles which she would take back home and use for creative craft work. She used to keep walking in search for the rightly shaped ones which could be of her use. This was one of her leisure activities in the evening. One evening, in her search, she had walked far away from home along the bank of the Mandh river and lost track of time.

The sun was setting and it was getting dark. She was late for home. Suddenly she heard her name from far away. It was her father, Gilloo, shouting from far away. Shakku realized that she was in for a good old scolding that evening. To avoid more trouble she ran towards her father. Gilloo agitatedly shouted at her, "What are you doing here so late? Come, let's go home." Shakku resisted by saying, "I wanna search for the stones for some more time." Gilloo denied her and both started walking back towards home. On her way Gilloo rested his hand on her daughter's shoulder and said. "My dear, you shouldn't be out here at this hour of the day. Aren't you aware that funerals are conducted on these river banks? In this tender age you should not see something which terrifies and gives you nightmares." Shakku was a 14-year old at that time.

When both of them reached home, Shakku's grandmother and mother were waiting for her. Her grandmother started scolding her first and then her mother joined in. It was becoming a long evening for Shakku but little did she know that the night would be even longer.

After having dinner with the family, Shakku was lying on the bed in her room trying to sleep. She couldn't help but overhear her grandmother and mother talking outside about the place where she had gone in the Mandh river.

[Sounds from the Living room:

Amma - “Do they still see those flames burning?”

....

Amma - “Those unrested souls....”

....

Sadho - “They take them to the spot where they died and ask to save them”]

Shakku thought why did she hear this spirit nonsense again. She will be afraid of the place which she enjoys and won't be able to stroll there alone and would miss her favorite evening leisure activity. Shakku had overheard part of the story and wanted to know more about it. She couldn’t ignore this further and rushed outside her room and questioned her elders about the topic.

Sadho scolded her for sneaking up on them and asked her to return to bed and try to sleep.

Shakku shook her head and said, “Tell me what are you talking about?” Sadho gave her a frowned look but realized at the same time that the kid won’t budge until she gets what she wants.

She made her sit close to her and narrated her the story, “It is about two sisters who went to swim in the Mandh river. They were accompanied by another girl who was the daughter of the servant in their home. All these three teenagers entered the river, but one of them went deep inside and far away from the banks."

"Suddenly, the water current increased and she was swept by the current. She shouted for help. The other two tried to save her but had the same fate and all of them drowned in the river at the same place and died. The people of the village were disheartened to see three young girls caught in this unfortunate event and losing their lives. Their hearts went out to the families who had lost their young children. An elder carrying out the last rites of a young one is a very painful and long ordeal. The families following the customs and traditions held the last rites properly."

Sadho further continued, "After this unfortunate event, shockingly few other persons were found to drown and die at the same place where these three teenagers had drowned. A handful who were saved reported that they felt as if someone was pulling them down holding their legs. It didn't take long for the villagers to realize that these new casualties at the same place could be linked to the first incident of the girls. Before the incident with the girls, no death of this sort had occured in the area. The belief that the souls of the three girls could be trapped in that area began to do the rounds. The villagers even went to the extent that they changed the course of the river stream, so that the place of incidence would be dry and in a hope that no more mishaps will happen. They wanted the three unrested souls to be free."

Even in the late night hours, Shakku was listening to her mother's narration without blinking her eyes. Sadho went on with the story saying, "The course of the river was redirected and the original site of the incident was now dry as it was planned. But after that other unbelievable incidents were being reported from the site. It was as if the souls were more agitated than ever. A few people reported that when they were crossing the bridge at that place, they saw three big rises of flames igniting in the night. Some reported that they saw three girls stopping their vehicle and asking them for help to save a girl who is drowning. All these occurrences were being reported from the same area where the unfortunate incident with the girls had happened. The villagers were frightened to visit the place after the sunset."

Sadho took a pause and said, "My dear, now you know the whole reason why we don't want you to be at that place during late evening hours. So, go to your bed and take a rest."

Shakku, who was scared after hearing the whole ordeal, hesitantly asked her mother, "Can I sleep with you tonight. I am scared to sleep alone after hearing all this." Sadho nodded and said, "See, this is the reason why I was not telling you the story in the first place."

Next day, Shakku asked her friends from the neighborhood about the story. She couldn't believe that everyone had heard about it and they knew everything all along. She felt stupid and dumb in a way. After some days she came to know that the river stream was restored to its original course and the villagers had assembled at the place and offered their prayers for the departed souls. She didn't bring up this matter in any further conversation and even tried hard to stop thinking about it.

Years passed and one day Shakku was returning from her residential school in Chandigarh in a car and crossing the bridge over the Mandh river. She noticed a shop at the place where the incidents were earlier reported. A stone-crusher was working on it. She was eighteen now and hadn't mentioned the incident for the past 4 years. Now, she got curious again and wanted to know what happened further. So, she asked her father about it. Her father told her that after the stone crusher has set-up his new shop there, no further unfortunate event has been reported. Whether it was because of him or someone else who finally brought those departed souls at peace nobody knows.

Shakku thought whether all the incidents at the site were because of the agitated souls and it was just the people trying to explain the events and connecting the dots. We come across many incidents which could not be explained rationally or logically. Whether they are co-incidences or one event is related to the other, who knows?

Story 9 - The Weeping Mother

In village lingo, it is said that, whenever a mother dies during pregnancy or after giving birth, the last rituals *(havan/yagna)* should be performed diligently as the departed soul can come back as it feels no one can take care of the child like she would. This can also haunt the whole village.

A pregnant lady in Shakku's neighbourhood died by committing suicide. Shakku, who was a 10 year old, overheard about the incident when her mother, Sadho and grandmother, Rani Devi were talking about it. Rani amma said to Sadho, "Poor lady has suffered an unnatural and painful death. God gives us life to live but we should not decide our end like this. She was carrying an unborn child also in her womb."

Sadho added to the incident, "Everyone in the village is saying that the *havan/yagna* (last rituals) should be done religiously or else she may come back and haunt the whole village". Rani amma continued further, "They will have to cut open the body to get the child out and perform rituals for both, the child as well the mother. They child should be close to her mother when both of them are leaving this place."

Later they came to know that the last rites in this case were done as required taking care of all the measures. The people of the village were also convinced that the souls were resting in peace.

Shakku, who overheard all this, got curious about this topic. What is this havan/yagna? What is done in this? What will happen if it is not done? And naturally she started poking her Amma, now and then, with many questions. Rani Amma realizing her grandchild was too young to hear about all this, dodged her questions by involving her in other chores.

Few months later, Rani Devi and Sadho came to know about a woman's death in a nearby village. The lady was pregnant and died after giving birth to a baby boy. She had a 5 year old girl child, before this boy. Her widowed husband was left with her daughter and a newborn baby boy. The husband did not believe in the Higher Power as he was kind of an atheist. He did not have faith in any of the religious practices which everyone used to prescribe. Hence, he went against the advice of the people at home and also the whole village, by not performing any last rites for his wife, who died an unnatural death.

The incident became the talk of the village and nearby places also. Few days into the event, the villagers started complaining that they were hearing the sound of crying & sobbing of a woman at night. Many villagers were having the same experience and it was an everyday happening. They believed these crying voices of the woman are nothing but the hauntings of the deceased mother who has come back for her child as she believes no one can take care of them better than her.

One more such incident was heard by Shakku. After the death of their mother, the newborn baby boy and the 5 year old girl of the deceased mother were taken care of by their grandmother. The two kids slept with their grandmother at night and the father in the other room of the house.

One night when all three were sleeping, the grandmother felt some touch on her body as though someone was searching for something. She was in a half sleep state and thought that the kids' father might have come from the other room to check on them. She felt the same thing almost every night.

However, one day she mentioned the same to his son in the morning. To her surprise, his son replied that he has never come to their room at night and definitely not touched anything. The same night when the scene repeated again, she woke up frightened to see nobody around and asked, " Who is it? Who are you? What do you want?". The reply which followed in a whispered voice petrified her, "My son is sleeping on the bed... And I am here to take him with me." She could make out that the voice was similar to that of the deceased mother. She narrated it to his son the next morning. She blamed him for going against the advice of everybody in the village and not carrying out the last rites sincerely.

These unexplainable events and many other things continued to occur in the house and the grandmother felt the kids were not safe at this place.

She conveyed the same to his son who now started wondering whether he was wrong in not doing the final rites as suggested by everyone. He also began fearing for his children.

When these incidents used to fall on Shakku's ears, she wondered why she had to pay attention to every ongoing conversation in the home. Her summer vacation was coming to an end and she had to go back to her boarding school. When she returned from boarding school on her next holiday, a year had passed, and she wanted to know what happened further in that incident. She asked her *Amma* regarding the same.

Her *Amma* told her that the cries of the poor soul are still heard in the neighborhood of that village. And the widower got married again recently. The man thought the new wife will be a solution to everything and she will take care of the home and the kids. He had sent the baby boy to her newly wedded wife's place thinking the kid would be safe there and time moved on.

Five years later, Shakku who was 16 now, returned from her residential High School in Chandigarh. She wanted to know about what had occurred further in that matter. She asked her Amma regarding the same who informed her that the people of that village had got used to cries of the weeping mother. Things were kind of getting back to normal.

The daughter of the deceased mother who was now of about 11 years was about to be sent to her Mausi's (Maternal Aunt's) place. The young girl was also having her school vacation and her father thought that she would have a change of place there and would enjoy her stay. She was excited to visit her aunt who always welcomed her with toys and sweets. She started packing her stuff for the stay and wore a red suit with a red-laced dupatta.

She even made a visit to Shakku's place. Shakku and Sadho (Shakku's mother) were seated in the courtyard when this young girl arrived. She greeted Sadho and Shakku with a namaste. After an exchange of sweets and conversations, the young girl left. Sadho was glad to see a child happy and was grateful that she is going to a place where she will be away from all the things and news she gets to hear here. She will be peaceful there.

The young girl was excited and she told everyone she met on the way that she was visiting her Mausi's (maternal aunt's) place. She waved goodbye to everyone and took the blessing of the elders. She completed her packing at home and just one more chore was left before her bus which was about to come at 6 pm in the evening.

She had to get the wheat grain from home grounded at the common machine where the whole village people used to get it done. She took the steel jar of grains to be used for the process and headed to the place. The people used to bring their wheat grains and paid money to use the machine. The machine was left unattended that time and this 11 year old girl was alone over there with her steel jar of grains. The owner of the place had another shop where groceries were sold and he was busy attending customers there.

The poor child tried to use the machine unsupervised which she had even done earlier. She started using the machine and after some time she felt her dupatta getting caught in the grinder. She tried to take it out but felt a stronger pull on the other side. What occured next scared her to the core. She heard the following in a whispered voice, "Come my child, Come! – Come to your Mother! I will take care of you!" Hearing this familiar voice, she made another attempt at an escape but with fail. She got pulled into the powerful grinder and lost her life.

The nearby villagers, hearing the loud scream of a girl, rushed to the place. They were shocked to see a beheaded body of a girl covered in a pool of blood and the head was not seen around. The Police were called to the place of incidence. There was no eye witness to the occurence. The grinding machine and the surrounding structures were covered in splashes of blood. The head was nowhere to be found which was a mystery for everyone.

Few moments later, when one from the Police Team opened the steel jar which the young girl had brought with her, the decapitated head of the poor child was found inside it, covered in wheat flour. The investigation couldn't uncover what had actually happened. Logic says that it surely must be a case of homicide. The girl must have been killed by somebody.

The father of the young girl got a second shock of his life to see her young daughter losing her life in such a tragedy. The frightful incident became the news of the village and surrounding areas. The incidence of a second unnatural death in the same family gave the people a lot to discuss about. The unfortunate father carried out the last rites of his girl child as per the rituals suggested by the elders of the village.

However, after that incident, the cries of the deceased weeping mother were no longer heard in the village. The people believed that it must have been the mother who came back from the dead for her child. She must have found her peace now.

The father moved to live with his new wife in her village. The 6 year old boy from his previous wife was also there. The three of them were on the bed soundly sleeping. Suddenly the man sees an image of his deceased wife and daughter and hears a familiar voice whispering, “I am coming for you and my child... All four of us will live here happily and in peace.” The man wakes up covered in sweat and frightened to his core.

Story 10 - Banmanus

The rains in Himachal turn the whole scenery into lush green landscapes. The heavy rains sometimes also lead to land erosions and landslides. The land receives rainfall from the months of July to September just like in the rest of India.

Shakku used to enjoy the rainy season and on her way back to home from school, she used to pick up *gucchi* (local name for an exotic variety of mushroom) and bring it home.

She had heard about an entity named *Ban-manus* (man of the forest). Her mother told her that if you ever encounter *Ban-manus* on the way then always run downhill.

She asked her mother, "Why downhill, maa?". Her mother answered, "He is a tall, human-like figure, with long white hair all over his face and body. If he starts chasing you and you run downhill, then his long hair will cover his eyes and it will be difficult for him to see you. Then you can easily make an escape and reach home safely."

Shakku wondered how does her mother know so much about this entity and that he keeps chasing people and other stuff. She questioned her mother and wanted to know more about this entity.

Her mother replied, "This being... he captures young girls. He has a lot of supernatural powers and captivates young females so that he can use them for procreation and make a family of his own" Shakku was amazed, "So, he takes away young girls". Sadho continued, "Yes, because of his supernatural powers, the young girl is not able to make an escape. He licks their feet and the girl is glued to the same place and doesn't feel like running away from there. He takes good care of the girl, nourishes her and impregnates her."

Sadho added, "My great grandmother told me an incident of a young girl who was taken away by this Ban-manus and returned after 9 months. She was found to be pregnant. When her family members asked her how she got pregnant and how she escaped? The girl replied that she was unhappy even after all his efforts and so the *Ban-manus* was kind enough to let her go and reunite with her family.

But she was carrying a child of the entity and he had made her promise that after the birth of the child, he would take it away the same night the baby was born." Shakku asked in surprise, "Wouldn't the family members of the girl were scared that the Ban-manus would be visiting them for his off-spring?"

Sadho answered, "He had told the girl to leave the baby in the courtyard outside the house at midnight. The people in the neighborhood believed that this was all a made-up story. The girl might have eloped with her lover who has left her now after impregnating her."

Sadho further continued, "But the night the baby was born, to everyone's surprise, he was not exactly a human. His body was fully covered in white hair and it was like a bear baby. The newborn didn't show any signs of life. The girl still did what she had promised to the *Ban-manus*.

She left the stillborn outside the house in the courtyard on a platform. Next morning, it was not there. After a period of about two weeks, scary echoes could be heard of a being who was bawling, howling and making sounds which no one would miss. Every year on the night when this entity was born, the same echoes could be heard. These howling and crowing sounds, although resembled human voices, were louder and far-reaching.

This went on for a few years on the same particular night when the newborn entity was delivered and died. Suddenly after a few years, the sounds could no longer be heard and the villagers thought that he might have had another baby or he must have moved out of the pain of losing an off-spring." Even in her tender age, all this was hard to believe for Shakku.

In her later years, Shakku had come across the stories of entities like BigFoot, Yeti and similar beings who are talked about across the globe in various parts. She wondered whether her mother's description of Ban-manus was the same as that of these beings seen in other regions of the world. No one has captured these beings on film.

Do they still exist in the mountains or have they vanished? Do they even exist?

There is a medical condition known as Hypertrichosis in which there is excessive hair growth. In a rare form of this condition known as "Werewolf syndrome", the person has excessive hair-growth all over the body, including the face. It is seen in both males and females but there are only a few cases across the globe. Could it be possible that these people are spotted as the mysterious entity... who knows?

Shakku had heard about Ban-manus from her grandmother too. She wondered how her grandmother was aware of all this when she didn't even read any books or there was not even a television in the house. When you apply logic to it, it is easier to believe that these stories are told as folks to young girls so that they don't run away with someone or are misguided. When an unmarried pregnant girl returns home, they use this entity as an explanation for the pregnancy.

So, illusion or fact? - It is for the reader to decide...

-x-x-x-

Story 11 - The Guest (‘*Prahunah*’)

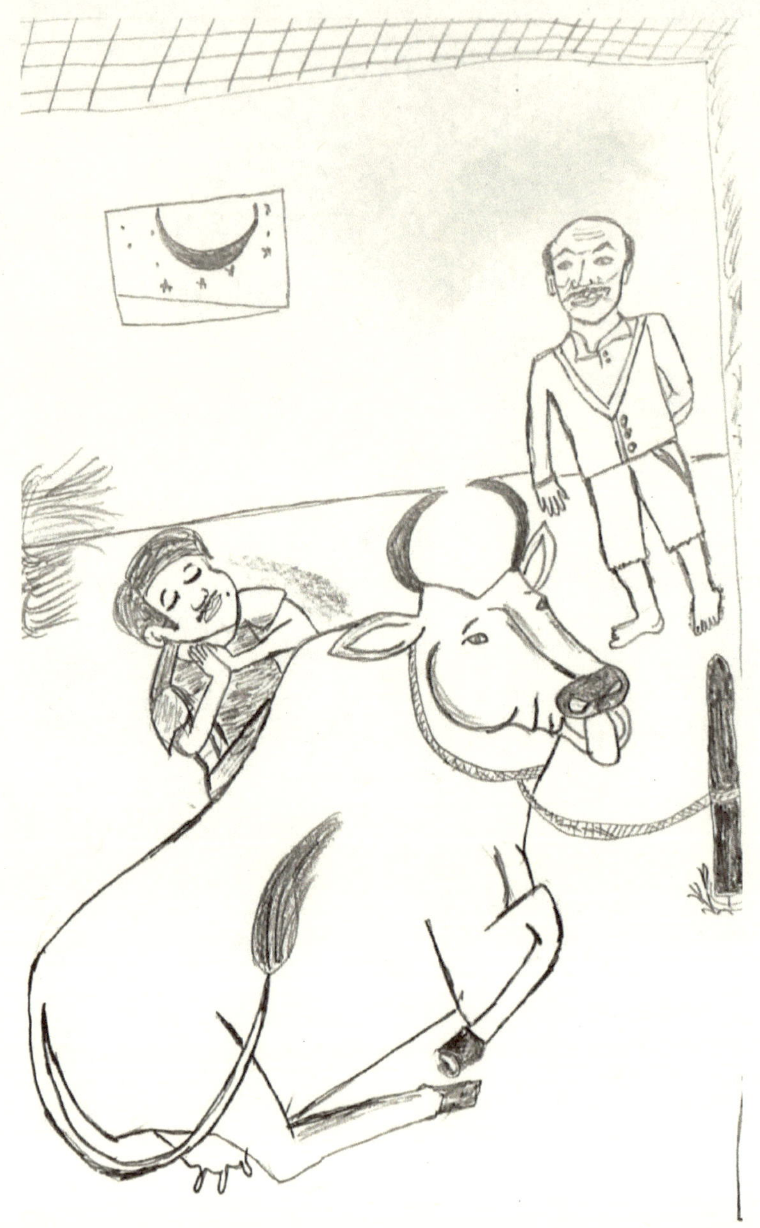

Shakku was having her summer vacation and she went to stay at her maternal uncle's house. The house was located in a dense forest area and she loved going there whenever an opportunity came. Her maternal grandmother and great grandmother also resided in that house. Her maternal great grandmother had an amazing collection of stories to narrate.

All the kids from the neighborhood thronged the place to listen to her stories and would spend the night there during vacation. It was a boon for the parents of the kids as the children would be nicely taken care of and the parents would have one less thing to worry about at their home.

Shakku's great grandmother (maternal) was a very responsible and respectful elderly woman in the village. She was entrusted with custody of the children and the parents would give permission to their children to spend the night at her place without any hesitation.

The children fondly addressed her as *Amma ji*. *Amma ji* was a versatile personality, irrespective of her age, she was even involved regularly in the house-hold chores and this made her hands a bit rough. She had this habit of constantly rubbing the back of the children while narrating her stories at night and it felt as if the back was being scrubbed by a pumice stone.

Among the whole lot of children, Shakku used to sit right next to her while sleeping at night. All the kids slept together in a vast single room with Amma ji. It was a calming and soothing experience for Shakku who often dozed off in the middle of the stories.

Among the many stories which *Amma ji* narrated, one was her most favorite and was equally loved by many other children and they never got tired of hearing that again and again. It was about the *Prahunah* (Sanskrit word for Guest). During the vacation of the children, one particular night, all the kids were lying on their beds arranged by Shakku's great grandmother (maternal) and children made a request for the story of The Guest. Shakku was lying on *Amma ji's* lap and her back was being patted as one does to put a child asleep. Amma ji took a long breath and started to narrate the following story.

A long time back there was a young adult man, Rahul, who went to visit his uncle, Suresh. Suresh was an elderly man in his 60s who was living all by himself in a remote area of Himachal Pradesh. He had a house on a farm with some cattle and horses. Suresh had no company in the place other than the farm animals. He had lost his wife during the middle-aged years and had one daughter who was married and living with her in-laws at a distant village. His house used to get surprise visitors in the form of loved ones, who came to check on and enquired about his well-being.

Rahul was a distant relative of his uncle, Suresh. During that time, Suresh's place was not well connected with landline phones and it was difficult to send a message to somebody for any news. Hence, Rahul had also visited without informing or sending a message.

Suresh used to cook delicious food on his own. He even made dairy products from the cattle produce like butter, curd, paneer and even sweet-derivatives of milk. He even hung natural honey (extracted with help of burning dry cow dung-smoke)in a pot of mud. The mud-pot hung from the top-shelf of the kitchen. The guests enjoyed their stay at his place.

Rahul had planned to stay for a day or two with his uncle. The main reason for the visit was to check on his health but he enjoyed the delicious food and even horse-riding in the village area. The walk for the house was a long 13 km from the main road. Rahul had started from his hometown on a bullock-cart. After reaching the main-road intersection of his uncle's village, he started enthusiastically on his feet to cover the 13 km to reach his uncle's place.

When he reached an uphill spot from where his uncle's house was in sight, he could see and hear the noise of the restless cattle outside the house. He got worried and started walking in a hurry towards the house. The sun was about to set and it was getting dark.

During his earlier visits, he often found his uncle on the porch in the courtyard of the house at this hour of the day. When he didn't see him outside, he called out for his uncle, "*Tauji*, where are you?" [*Tauji* is a formal address for a paternal uncle who is elder to one's father]

Suresh replied from his room in the house, "I am here, Rahul *beta* (my child)...". He added, "I am not feeling well today... so I am lying on the bed in my room. Please, come inside..."

Rahul heaved a sigh of relief as he was worried about his uncle. Seeing the cattle roaming outside unanchored at this hour was not a usual sight. By this time usually, the cattle were tied to their place and even milking of the cows was done in this evening time. By learning about his uncle's condition, he was feeling sad for him but at the same time a part of him wanted to enjoy the visit. He felt he won't get the special attention this time to which he was used to earlier as a guest.

Holding this thought, he entered the house and went to his uncle's room. He had brought some Indian blackberrys (Java plum) from his hometown for his uncle. Suresh was not even able to sit and welcomed his nephew lying down. After an initial conversation and a few catching up on things, Rahul left the room to tie the cattle to their place and even milked them for a liter of milk. One particular white cow, Gauri, was his favorite among the lot and he gently stroked her back and went back in the house.

On returning to his uncle's room, he was feeling very hungry as he had made a long journey to reach Suresh's house. He politely asked his uncle, "Tauji, Is there anything in the house which is ready to eat?" Suresh replied, "I have recently extracted a good portion of fresh honey. Let me get that for you."

Suresh Uncle stretched his arm which now not only could touch the roof but had become long enough to reach the kitchen. The long arm brought the pot of honey from the kitchen and it was retracting and getting shorter as it was coming back.

Rahul was stunned and was about to faint watching the horrific act. He somehow managed to control his response and tried to act normal.

He even took a spoon of honey and ate it and complimented his uncle about the taste of it in a stammering voice. Deep down he was trying to get a hold of the situation. He noticed that his uncle wasn't breathing normally as there were no chest or abdominal movements. He even realized that when he had touched his uncle' feet earlier to greet him and take his blessings, the feet were stone-cold to touch as in the case of a deceased corpse. Rahul came to the conclusion that his uncle is no more and his body is being possessed by a ghost or something supernatural. He was trapped in a house with an unknown entity that too at the hour of the night. He had to somehow let the night pass and survive also.

Amma ji noticed that Shakku was half-asleep at this stage and so she told the rest of the kids that she will continue with the story tomorrow. Just then one of the kids gently kicked Shakku to wake her up.

Amma mannered him up and told him that one should not behave like this and also realized that there will be a fight now if she doesn't complete the story. So she continued with the story of The Guest.

Rahul told his uncle Suresh (talking dead man lying on bed) that he needed to go to the toilet and left the room. He went to the place where the cattle were tied. There he sat next to the white cow, Gauri. He prayed to his favorite cow to let him survive the night and protect him. He hid behind the cow praying to God and his ancestors.

At the hour of midnight, the dead corpse of his Uncle came calling Rahul's name and reached the area where the cattle were tied. He uttered, "My son, I have lived my life all alone and now I feel the need of someone, to be accompanied with, in the path after death." Rahul couldn't believe his eyes and ears to what he saw next. Gauri, the cow, started talking. The cow responded to the dead corpse, "I will definitely tell you where Rahul is... But first you will have to count the number of hairs in my tail correctly." The corpse agreed to what Gauri, the cow, demanded and started counting the number of hairs. Just when a few hairs were left to count, Gauri would sway its tail and the possessed body of Suresh had to begin the counting again. This went on all night and Rahul was safely hiding among the herd of cattle being a spectator of this unbelievable episode and praying for his life.

The sun was about to rise and before the first rays could hit the earth, the dead corpse of Suresh went back to its original place in the bedroom. Rahul realized the night of terror had passed and Gauri, the cow had saved his life. He thanked the cow and rushed to a nearby house which was 3 km away. He ran barefoot and narrated the ordeal of the previous night to the neighbor, Bappi.

Bappi, a man in his 40s, was stunned and said that he saw Rahul's uncle yesterday afternoon. He had come to know that Suresh was no more and had sent the message to his daughter who was on her way to this village. Since the evening was about to come and it was getting darker, he had left the body alone and didn't expect that any one would visit.

Bappi had a doubt regarding Rahul's portrayal of events. But his queries were resolved when he saw that feet of the dead body of Suresh were mud-stained and covered in cow-dung. Yesterday when he had seen them they were clear. Also, when he visited the cattle area, there were marks of Suresh's feet around.

Suresh's daughter and husband reached the place and even they were shocked to hear what Rahul had gone through the previous night.

All the kids were hearing the story with their eyes wide-open. Amma ji concluded her narration by adding, "This is the reason why, to this day, people are afraid to go to somebody's house as an uninvited guest." The kids were in a terrified state and sleep was a distant thing for them even if they were hearing this story for the 10th time.

During her adulthood, Shakku reflected on this story and thought that this story is told to children so that they learn an important message that one should not go to anybody's place uninvited. The narration also teaches that one should not leave their elders alone or abandon them, but should be with them and take care of them. The story also highlights the importance of a cow in the life of humans. A cow not only provides milk but is a creature of spiritual and religious importance in Hinduism. Be it any animal, a human should not just think of his own existence but the well-being of all the species on the earth.

Glossary of Terms used in the Book

Shakku - name of the girl child who is the central character in all the stories

Sadho - name of Shakku's mother

Rani Devi - name of Shakku's grandmother

Amma - way to address one's grandmother in pahadi and many other languages

Gilloo - name of Shakku's father

Dharmu - name of Shakku's Uncle

Chaleda - *Chaleda* is a *Pahadi* language word for some who does '*chal*' (tricks). The word is used for an entity labeled as the trickster in a story. It is similar to other fictional supernatural characters as shape-shifters or drifters.

Gaura - name of the family owned cow at Shakku's home

Pahadiya - an entity residing in the Peepal (Sacred Fig) tree. It is a tall being and wears white clothes. He is both worshiped as well as feared. The people make their offerings to this local deity in white color like - cooked white rice, white flowers, white flags

Bataali - it is a creature who lives deep inside the naturally formed water-caves in the Himalayas (fictional entity). Its whole body is covered with fish-like scales.

Ban-manus - a fictional entity existing hiddenly in the forest of the hilly area. Its whole body is covered with hair and it is a tall creature. It is similar to other fictional characters like the Yeti and Bigfoot.

***Peepal* (Sacred Fig) Tree** - Peepal is a tree that has been revered since the beginning of civilization and has a wide range of medicinal properties in addition to its religious significance. Ashwattha is another name for the peepal tree. In Hinduism, the tree is revered as a holy tree. Vasudeva, Chaitanya, and world tree are some of the other names for the peepal tree.According to Hindu mythology, Lord Brahma lives in the peepal tree's roots, Lord Vishnu lives in the peepal tree's trunk, and Lord Shiva lives in the peepal tree's leaves. (source of information: ganeshaspeaks.com)

Jin - a local language word for Jeanie

Prahunah - sanskrit word for ‘Guest’

Acknowledgement

The author/s are grateful to Dr Satotsna Patra who has edited and proofread this work. She is working as a Pathologist in Bhubaneswar and is the first reader of this book. Her valuable inputs have made the final output more polished before publishing it in the public domain.

Most of the sketches used in this book are done by author Dr Shagun Thakur herself. The sketches of 'The Trickster' and 'Bataali in the Kund' are drawn by Dr Ananya Nath whereas the sketch of 'Fires of the Angry Soul' is made by Dr Roshni Nayak; both of them are interns in a medical college at Bhubaneswar. The sketch of 'The Bird-chirp' is made by Mr. Vinay from Himachal Pradesh. The author/s are grateful to them for providing well-made sketches in a timely manner.

The author ,Dr Shagun Thakur, is also grateful to be born and brought up in Himachal Pradesh from where she got the inspiration to design the concept and the stories of this book.

Foreword

The authors are thankful to the readers for showing their interest in this book. They are hopeful that the readers enjoyed reading the stories as much as the authors who spent their time and energy in creating this work of fiction.

A review from the reader at the place of purchase of this book will go a long way in the success of the book and authors would be grateful for that.

If the reader wishes to share their personal experiences about any similar supernatural/ unexplainable event, he/she can reach the author at drshagunthakur@gmail.com

Thank you!

www.ingramcontent.com/pod-product-compliance
Lightning Source LLC
LaVergne TN
LVHW041113150826
845673LV00007B/2034